'Mr Forbes said' – she hesitated, then went on as though the words were wrenched out of her throat, 'he told me that there were – children.'

'We – I have a four-year-old daughter and a baby son.'

The girl's eyes darkened. She drew in her breath sharply, then said in a burst of anguished rage, 'I wish he knew how much misery he's caused with his selfishness! I wish I could tell him! He's ruined everything for me – for us!'

Tears sparkled among her lashes, diamonds in a mesh of gold, and Isla automatically stretched a comforting hand across the table towards her. Ainslie jerked back, rising to her feet with an awkward motion that set the china on the table jangling and the tea slopping in the cups.

'Don't touch me!'

'My dear—'

'Keep away from my mother! Keep out of Paisley!' Ainslie McAdam blurted the words, her face crumpling, then almost ran out of the room, heedless of the faces that turned to watch her go then swung back to where Isla sat, alone, at the table.

McAdam's Women

Evelyn Hood

WARNER BOOKS

A *Warner* Book

First published in Great Britain in 1994
by Little, Brown and Company
This edition published in 1995 by Warner Books

Copyright © Evelyn Hood, 1994

The moral right of the author has been asserted.

*All characters in this publication are fictitious and
any resemblance to real persons, living or dead,
is purely coincidental.*

A CIP catalogue record for this book
is available from the British Library

ISBN 0 7515 0841 1

Typeset by M Rules
Printed and bound in Great Britain by
Clays Ltd, St Ives plc

Warner Books
A Division of
Little, Brown and Company (UK)
Brettenham House
Lancaster Place
London WC2E 7EN

1

Although she had been watching the doorway intently for the past five minutes, Isla felt a sense of shock, like a fist slamming into her breastbone, when the girl she had been expecting arrived. They had never set eyes on each other before, but she would have known immediately who the newcomer was, even if they had only glanced at each other in a crowded street in passing.

From beneath a black cloche hat clear blue eyes swept the busy tearoom, halting as they reached the table in the corner, and Isla's tentative, half-raised hand.

They flared, just as Kenneth's did whenever he was astonished. Black-gloved fingers reached out to grasp the door-frame for a moment, and then, wiping the shock from her face with a deliberate effort, the girl came across the room, skirting tables, side-stepping waitresses.

Isla had intended to rise to meet her, but instead she stayed where she was, pinned to the small chair by this reminder of her recent loss. The paralysing agony had hit her several times since Kenneth's death; just as she thought that she had accepted it and come to terms with it, sudden realisation and a wave of desolation swept anew through her.

1

Now her first sight of Kenneth's daughter – his older daughter – had revived it.

The girl had his clear, steady, somewhat pale blue eyes, though in her case they were fringed with gold, instead of Kenneth's more stubby lashes. She had his strongly marked brows, his mouth – without, of course, the red-gold moustache above it – his straight neat nose. Beneath the black velvet hat she wore, Isla glimpsed hair the vibrant glowing bronze of autumn leaves. The colour Kenneth's had been. Her face was oval, her chin neatly rounded where his had been square. Slim and straight, dressed in a high-necked black knitted suit, black stockings, black shoes, she even had Kenneth's walk, lithe and quick and easy, though constricted at that moment by the tables in the room.

Isla's throat tightened, and for a moment tears prickled behind her eyes. She fought them back, telling herself sternly that she was not going to let herself weep in this public place, in front of this young woman who looked so familiar to her, yet was a stranger.

Swallowing hard, she regained her own self-control as the girl arrived beside her table, suddenly hesitant and unsure. 'You can't be—' she began, then stopped, folding her mouth round the next two words as though to hold them back.

Isla got to her feet. 'I'm Isla Mc—' She hesitated, then said clearly, 'Isla McAdam.'

The girl's eyes flared again, this time with arrogant anger, and she ignored the hand that was held out to her. 'You've got no right to that name!'

'Please believe me when I say that I thought I had,'

Isla said steadily, letting her hand fall back to her side. 'And you're Ainslie.'

'But you're so young!'

'I'm twenty-six.' Twenty-six for the past week. Her birthday had come one short week after hearing of Kenneth's death.

'My God!' There was anger in Ainslie's voice. 'You're only five years older than I am – and he was forty-six!' She swayed slightly, groped for the back of a chair, found it, and sank into it.

'I knew Kenneth's age, but I never felt that it mattered.' Isla took her own seat again, still fighting to keep her voice level. She had made up her mind that she wasn't going to be afraid of this girl, but despite herself, the fear was there. Without knowing it, she had been part of a terrible wrong committed against Ainslie McAdam and her mother and brother.

Colour rose to Ainslie's cheeks and contempt honed her voice. 'How could he do this to – to us?'

It was numbing to look into eyes so like Kenneth's, yet cold in a way his had never been. Under his daughter's antagonistic stare Isla might well have given way to her grief and her terror of the unknown future, but it was the contemptuous note in the girl's voice that saved her from possible weakness. She wasn't to blame for what had happened, she had nothing to be ashamed of. She would not allow this young woman to make her feel like a criminal.

'Ainslie – Miss McAdam, it was you who suggested this meeting. If you've changed your mind, you're free to go, though I've ordered tea for us both.'

It arrived just at that moment, brought to them by a

3

middle-aged woman so plump that her small white frilled apron looked like a postage stamp stuck on to her black dress. She deftly transferred the cups and saucers and the nickel-plated teapot and sugar bowl and milk jug to the spotless white table-cloth, then scurried to a huge sideboard and brought back a tiered plate-stand filled with plates of cakes and biscuits. Her eyebrows rose and she looked hurt when Ainslie McAdam impatiently flapped a hand at her and said, 'Take these away!'

'Madam? The cakes've just come up fresh from the bakery below . . .'

Isla forced the corners of her lips into a placating smile. 'They look delicious, but I don't think we're in the mood for them today.'

The woman's eyes swept from one to the other, taking in Ainslie's black suit and the black armband on the sleeve of Isla's grey woollen coat. Her own face fell into solemn lines.

'Of course, madam,' she murmured, and went off, leaving them alone and silent in a roomful of chattering, brightly dressed women.

Ainslie McAdam watched, her brows drawn together in a straight line above brooding eyes, as Isla drew off her gloves and began to pour tea. She shook her head when Isla lifted the milk jug, and pulled her own gloves off, lifting a hand to flick the flowing end of the black silk scarf that served as a hatband back from her shoulder.

Carefully, aware of the unblinking gaze opposite, Isla poured her own tea, added milk and more sugar than she would normally have taken, and stirred the liquid. The hot sweet tea helped to steady her nerves.

'This is very difficult for us both,' she said as she returned the cup to its saucer.

'I asked you to meet me here because I won't have you calling on my mother. She's never been strong, and now she's ill with worry and shame over this – this business. I'll not have her upset any further!'

'I've no intention of forcing myself on your mother, or on any other member of your family.'

Ainslie's eyes said that she didn't believe that. 'Why would you come here to Paisley if you weren't out to make trouble for us?'

'I came at my——', Isla stopped herself just in time from saying, 'my husband's', and changed it to, 'your father's lawyer's invitation. There are matters we have to discuss.'

'You – talk to his lawyer?' Ainslie's voice rose, and one or two people at neighbouring tables turned to look at the two sombrely dressed young women. She noticed the curious glances, and lowered her tone. 'But there's nothing to talk about. You weren't his wife!'

The words stung against Isla's cheeks like small stones, raising spots of colour. 'I thought I was.'

'You thought wrong!'

'I know that now. And I didn't ask Mr Forbes for this meeting – as I said, I'm in Paisley at his invitation.'

'I don't see why,' Ainslie McAdam said with open hostility.

'Nor do I, until I see him.'

Ainslie's right hand, having dealt with the trouble-some hat-ribbon, was rubbing nervously at the third finger of her left hand. Her gaze dipped to the gold band on Isla's wedding finger, and her mouth tightened.

'Mr Forbes said' – she hesitated, then went on as though the words were wrenched out of her throat, 'he told me that there were – children.'

'We – I have a four-year-old daughter and a baby son.'

The girl's eyes darkened. She drew in her breath sharply, then said in a burst of anguished rage, 'I wish he knew how much misery he's caused with his selfishness! I wish I could tell him! He's ruined everything for me – for us!'

Tears sparkled among her lashes, diamonds in a mesh of gold, and Isla automatically stretched a comforting hand across the table towards her. Ainslie jerked back, rising to her feet with an awkward motion that set the china on the table jangling and the tea slopping in the cups.

'Don't touch me!'

'My dear—'

'Keep away from my mother! Keep out of Paisley!' Ainslie McAdam blurted the words, her face crumpling, then almost ran out of the room, heedless of the faces that turned to watch her go then swung back to where Isla sat, alone, at the table.

She reached for her cup and discovered that she was trembling so much that she had to use both hands to lift it from the saucer. Head bowed, she sipped at the tea again, but now its warmth held no comfort for her. The waitress appeared as she put the cup down, her face creased with concern.

'Is something wrong, madam? Isn't your friend coming back? She's scarcely touched her tea.'

'No, she's not coming back.'